Bella
the Bunny
Fairy

For Evie Tolley, a wonderful
fairy goddaughter

Special thanks to
Narinder Dhami

No part of this work may be reproduced, stored in a retrieval system,
or transmitted in any form or by any means, electronic,
mechanical, photocopying, recording, or otherwise, without
written permission of the publisher. For information regarding permission, write to Rainbow Magic Limited, c/o HIT Entertainment,
830 South Greenville Avenue, Allen, TX 75002-3320.

ISBN-10: 0-545-04185-6
ISBN-13: 978-0-545-04185-0

12 11   10 11 12 13 14/0

Printed in the U.S.A.   40

First Scholastic printing, March 2008

Bella
the Bunny
Fairy

by Daisy Meadows

SCHOLASTIC INC.

New York   Toronto   London   Auckland

Sydney   Mexico City   New Delhi   Hong Kong

Jack Frost's
Ice Castle

Bramble
Stables

Jane Dillon's House

ark

rsty's
ouse

Jamie
Cooper's
House

The
Wainwrights'
House

Fairies with their pets I see
and yet no pet has chosen me!
So I will get some of my own
to share my perfect frosty home.

This spell I cast, its aim is clear:
to bring the magic pets straight here.
The Pet Fairies soon will see
their seven pets living with me!

Contents

Easter Bunny

"Isn't it a perfect day for a party?"
Kirsty Tate asked, looking up at the
sapphire-blue sky.

Her best friend, Rachel Walker,
nodded and handed Kirsty a chocolate
egg. Rachel was staying with Kirsty for
spring vacation, and the girls were busy
hiding eggs. They were getting ready

for an Easter party for Jane, Mr. and Mrs. Dillon's five-year-old daughter. The Dillons lived down the street from Kirsty.

"There are some great hiding places here," Rachel said. She gazed around the beautiful yard full of green grass and colorful flower beds. Then she knelt down and hid the egg under a shrub. "Jane and her friends will love the Easter egg hunt!"

"It'll be fun," Kirsty agreed, hiding an egg behind the birdbath.

"How many kids are invited to the party?" Rachel asked.

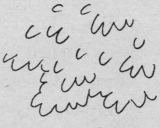

"Eleven!" Kirsty replied, her eyes twinkling. "Mr. and Mrs. Dillon are so glad that we're helping out! They've been friends with my mom and dad for a long time, and Jane is really sweet." Then she lowered her voice. "Do you think we'll find another one of the missing fairy pets today, Rachel?"

"I hope so," Rachel whispered back. "Let's keep our eyes open!"

Rachel and Kirsty had a special secret. They were best friends with the fairies! Whenever there was trouble in Fairyland, the girls were always happy to help. But trouble usually meant that mean Jack Frost and his goblins were up to no good.

This time, Jack Frost had been angry because he didn't have a pet of his own. He had kidnapped the seven magical animals belonging to the Pet Fairies! The pets had all been taken to his ice castle, but the mischievous animals had escaped into the human world. Jack Frost then sent his goblins to capture the pets and bring them back!

Without their magic animals, the Pet

Fairies couldn't help pets in the human world that were lost or in danger. The girls were determined to find the fairy pets before Jack Frost's goblins did!

"Well, we've gotten off to a good start," Kirsty pointed out. "Katie the Kitten Fairy was so happy when we returned her magic kitten, Shimmer."

Just then, a pretty little girl with long

blond curls waved from the back door. "Hi, Kirsty! Hi, Rachel!" she called. Jane had been upstairs changing into her pink party dress when the girls arrived. Now she rushed toward them, her face bright with excitement.

"All of my friends are coming to the party, Kirsty! We're going to have an Easter egg hunt, and then Mommy and Daddy are giving me a special Easter present!" she said breathlessly.

"You're so lucky, Jane!" Kirsty smiled as Mr. and Mrs. Dillon followed their daughter out into the yard.

"Jane, let's go get the presents ready for your guests," said Mrs. Dillon, noticing

that Rachel and Kirsty still had some chocolate eggs to hide. "I think Rachel and Kirsty are busy!"

She and Jane went back inside, and Mr. Dillon turned to the girls. "It's really nice of you to help out," he said gratefully. "There's so much to do." Then he smiled. "Would you like to see Jane's Easter present?"

The girls both nodded, and Mr. Dillon led them to the garage. Inside, sitting on the workbench, was a cardboard box with little holes in it. Rachel and Kirsty peeked inside and saw a fluffy black rabbit with floppy ears, nestled on a bed of straw.

"Oh, it's so cute!" Rachel gasped.

"Jane will love it," Kirsty added.

Mr. Dillon smiled. "Yes, she will," he agreed. "She's been pestering us for a rabbit!"

Rachel turned to Kirsty. "We'd better finish hiding the eggs," she said. "The guests will be here soon! Thanks for showing us the surprise, Mr. Dillon."

Quickly, the girls hid the remaining eggs behind flowerpots, trees, and the shed. Just as Kirsty placed the last egg behind a clump of daffodils, she heard the front doorbell ring.

"Here they come!" Rachel said with a grin.

Fifteen minutes later, all the guests had arrived. Jane was dashing around the garden with her friends, looking for the chocolate eggs.

"I found one!" Jane shouted, her cheeks glowing.

"Good job!" Kirsty laughed. She and Rachel were watching from the patio. There were shrieks of delight as some of the other children found eggs, too.

"Oh!" A little girl in a yellow dress suddenly gasped loudly. "Come look!"

Rachel and Kirsty hurried over to the girl. She was kneeling down in front of a tree, peering at the trunk.

"I just saw the Easter Bunny!" she announced breathlessly.

Rachel and Kirsty stared at her, confused. They hadn't hidden a toy rabbit anywhere!

"Where?" asked Rachel.

The little girl pointed at a hole in the tree trunk. "It came out of there, but then it popped back in again," she said.

"How do you know it was the Easter Bunny?" Kirsty asked.

"Because it was bright pink!" the little girl replied.

Rachel and Kirsty glanced at each other in surprise. Then Rachel looked more closely at the hole in the tree. Suddenly, her heart began to race. She was sure she could see the faintest glimmer of fairy magic!

Vanishing Act

Rachel nudged Kirsty, who had just sent the little girl off to search for more eggs. "Look!" she whispered.

Kirsty stared at the shimmering, magical haze in front of the tree trunk, and her eyes lit up. "Fairy magic!" She gasped. "Rachel, do you think —"

But before Kirsty could finish, there was another shout from across the yard.

"I saw the Easter Bunny, too!" A little boy was pointing at a large, leafy shrub and beaming with pride.

Kirsty and Rachel ran over to him. They could hardly believe their eyes. There was a beautiful, fluffy lilac-colored rabbit, sitting under the shrub! But as Kirsty bent to move the leaves out of the way, the rabbit vanished in a glittering cloud of purple sparkles.

"This is definitely fairy magic!"

Kirsty whispered. "The bunny must be one of the fairy pets!"

"Yes, I'll bet it's Bella the Bunny Fairy's rabbit!" Rachel agreed.

By now, all the children wanted to see the Easter Bunny.

"Where did the bunny go?" asked one little girl, looking disappointed.

"I don't know," Kirsty replied quickly. "Why don't you go and look for more eggs until we find out?"

"Let's look for the Easter Bunny instead!" Jane suggested. All the children cheered. They began racing around the yard, calling, "Bunny! Where are you?"

"We have to find the rabbit and get it back to Bella," Kirsty whispered to Rachel. "Luckily, I don't see any goblins around! I wonder where the bunny is now?"

Suddenly, Rachel's eyes widened. She grabbed her friend's arm. "Look at the picnic table!"

Mr. and Mrs. Dillon had put the party food out on the table while the children searched for eggs. They had just gone back inside to get more.

But as the girls stared, they could see a swirl of golden sparkles hovering over the food!

The girls hurried to the table. Sitting next to a big plate of salad, nibbling on a carrot, was the magic bunny. And now, it was a sunshine-yellow color!

Before Kirsty and Rachel could do anything, Jane spotted the rabbit, too.

"The Easter Bunny!" she shouted. The whole group of children rushed over to the table.

"Be careful," Rachel said anxiously. Would the bunny disappear again if it got scared?

But Jane stepped up to the table and gently stroked the rabbit's fluffy head. It seemed quite happy to have someone pet it.

"Isn't it cute?" Jane said with a sigh. "I wish I had my very own bunny!"

"We'd better get the rabbit away before Mr. and Mrs. Dillon come back out," Kirsty whispered to Rachel. "I don't know how we'll explain a yellow bunny! We can take it over to my house."

Rachel nodded. "The bunny's very tired," she announced to Jane and her friends, picking it up gently. "It's going home now, so say good-bye."

"Good-bye, Easter Bunny!" the children cried, waving. Then they dashed off to search for more Easter eggs.

"I'll tell the Dillons we have to run home for something," Kirsty murmured to Rachel, heading inside.

When she came back outside, the two girls carried the bunny around the house. They went out through the side gate and closed it carefully behind them. "How are we going to keep the rabbit safe until Bella the Bunny Fairy gets here?" asked Rachel as the girls walked along an overgrown path next to the house. "She can't be far away," Kirsty replied. "But maybe we could use the fairy dust in our magic lockets to take the bunny back to Fairyland ourselves."

Before Rachel could reply, the girls heard a nasty chuckling sound above their heads. Alarmed, they looked up. Four green goblins were sitting on the branch of a large oak tree, grinning down at them!

"Oh, no!" Rachel gasped.

"Let's get out of here!" Kirsty whispered.

The two girls hurried along the path. But all of a sudden, the ground beneath their feet seemed to disappear.

"Help!" Kirsty cried as she tumbled into a large hole.

Rachel was too shocked to yell, but luckily she managed to keep hold of the magic rabbit as she fell. The two girls landed on a bed of soft leaves and looked at each other in horror.

"The goblins must have dug this hole and covered it with branches." Kirsty gasped. "They set a trap!"

"And we walked right into it!" Rachel groaned.

"Ha, ha, ha!" the goblins cackled gleefully, peering down at the girls.

"We were trying to catch the magic bunny, but we also caught two pesky girls!" one goblin cried. "Hooray!"

Bella Flies In

As Rachel and Kirsty climbed to their
feet, the goblins bent over the hole.
Before the girls could stop them, one
of the goblins reached down and snatched
the magic rabbit out of Rachel's
hands. The bunny squirmed in dismay.

"Give that bunny back!" Rachel
shouted, trying to climb up out of the hole.

"Come and get it!" jeered the goblins. They ran around the side of the house toward the front yard, laughing and cheering as they went.

"We can't let them get away!" Kirsty said urgently, trying to pull herself out of the hole, too. But it was just a *little* too deep for the girls to climb out of.

Just then, a silvery voice echoed through the air. "Hang on, girls, I'm coming!"

Rachel and Kirsty looked up. A tiny fairy surfed through the air toward them on a large green oak leaf. Her long hair streamed out behind her in the breeze.

"It's Bella the Bunny Fairy!" Kirsty said happily. Bella came to a stop above Rachel's and Kirsty's heads and waved at them. She wore a beautiful green dress, beaded sunflowers at her waist and neck, and gold shoes.

"We're so glad to see you, Bella,"
Rachel said gratefully. "But I'm afraid
the goblins have run off with your
bunny. We're so sorry!"

Bella nodded. "I knew Misty
was around here
somewhere!" she
exclaimed.
"Don't worry,
those goblins
can't have gone
far. I'll have you
girls out of there
in two twitches of
a bunny's nose!"

She lifted her wand, and a shower
of golden sparkles floated down onto
the girls.

Rachel and Kirsty held their breath as they shrank to fairy size, and glittering wings appeared on their backs.

"Great idea, Bella!" Rachel laughed as she flew easily out of the hole, with Kirsty beside her.

"What should we do now?" asked Kirsty. The three friends hovered in midair, wings fluttering. "How will we find the goblins?"

Just then, a gruff, angry shout rang out across the yard.

"Follow that sound!" Bella cried, swooping through the air toward the front of the house.

Rachel and Kirsty hurried behind her. Within moments, the three of them peered around the corner of the house, into the front yard.

The goblins were crouched behind some bushes under an open window. They were arguing fiercely. One of

them, the biggest goblin, was holding Misty.

"There's my bunny!" Bella whispered, pointing at the frightened-looking rabbit. "Girls, we have to save her!"

Bunnies Everywhere!

The goblins hadn't noticed Rachel, Kirsty, and Bella watching them. They were too busy arguing.

"You do it!" one snarled.

"No, you do it!" another replied.

"I'm not climbing up there!" The first goblin said, pointing at the open window. "I might fall and hurt myself!"

"Coward!" jeered the goblin holding Misty.

"What are they arguing about?" Rachel whispered.

"Look!" Kirsty replied, pointing at the open kitchen window. A big basket of chocolate Easter eggs sat on the windowsill. "You know how greedy the goblins are. They want those chocolate eggs!"

Under the window was a wooden
trellis with roses growing on it. One of
the goblins tried to climb the trellis,
but it swayed slightly. He
jumped off, nervous.

"What's the matter
with you?" another
goblin sneered.
"Scaredy-cat!"

"Am not!" the
climbing goblin
roared furiously.

"Poor Misty!" Bella
said, staring anxiously at
her bunny. "She's shaking
with fear."

"Why can't she just disappear, like she
did before?" asked Kirsty.

Bella shook her head sadly. "Misty

can't disappear if someone's holding her, or if she's scared," she explained. "We have to figure out a way to get her back!"

While Kirsty and Bella were talking, Rachel had been looking at the basket of chocolate eggs. In the middle of it sat a beautiful, blue toy bunny. It looked a lot like Misty! Just then, Rachel had an idea.

Excited, she turned to the little fairy. "Bella, I think there might be a way to get back Misty!

Can you make me and Kirsty human-size again?"

Bella nodded. She waved her wand, and in an instant the two girls were back to normal.

"We need to go inside the house," Rachel whispered.

Confused, Kirsty and Bella followed Rachel back to the side gate. As Rachel opened it, Bella fluttered down and hid in her pocket. Then the girls walked into the backyard, where the children were still looking for eggs.

Mr. and Mrs. Dillon were putting plates out on the picnic table.

"Mrs. Dillon, is it OK if I borrow the blue bunny from the Easter egg basket in the kitchen? I promise to return it," Rachel asked.

Mrs. Dillon looked surprised, but she said it was all right.

Rachel and Kirsty smiled at her and went inside to the kitchen. Rachel peeked out the window and saw the goblins still arguing down below. Then she picked up the blue toy bunny and gave the basket a little tap. A few of the chocolate eggs fell out and tumbled to the ground outside the window.

"That'll keep the goblins busy for a few more minutes!" Rachel said quietly.

Kirsty looked out over the windowsill. The goblins had pounced on the chocolate eggs and were gobbling them up.

"Let's head back outside now," Rachel whispered. Kirsty followed her friend out of the house, through the side gate, and over to the hole in the path that the goblins had made.

"Kirsty, can you cover the hole with twigs and leaves like the goblins did?" Rachel asked.

Kirsty nodded and began pulling some fallen branches over the hole.

"Bella, we need a long piece of string," said Rachel. "Can you help?"

"Of course!" Bella agreed, zooming out of Rachel's pocket. She waved her wand. In a shower of sparkles, a long piece of golden string appeared on the path.

Rachel grabbed the string. She tied one end of it around the middle of the blue toy bunny. Kirsty and Bella watched in amazement. They didn't have a clue what Rachel was up to!

"We're all set!" Rachel grinned as she finished tying the knot. "Now all we need is Misty's help to make sure my plan works!"

Goblin Chase!

"Tell me what Misty has to do," Bella said eagerly.

"We need her to escape from the goblins for a few minutes," Rachel explained, waving the toy bunny in the air. "Then we'll try to confuse them with this!"

"You mean, we'll make the goblins think the toy is Misty?" Kirsty said. "But to do that, Misty will need to be —"

"Blue!" Bella laughed. "No problem!" Lifting her wand, she began to write in the air with it. Like a sparkler, the wand left a glittering trail of bright blue letters, the exact same color as the toy bunny. The letters spelled out:

TURN

BLUE

"Perfect!" Rachel declared, grinning.

"Now Misty knows exactly what color blue she has to be!" Bella said with a smile. As the words hovered in midair, she flicked her wand and sent them floating around the side of the house, toward her pet. The girls followed, eager to see what would happen. They could hear the goblins squabbling loudly.

"That's mine! Give it back!"

"You've had lots, greedy guts!"

"Who are you calling greedy guts?"

The goblins were still fighting over the chocolate eggs. Rachel and Kirsty peeked around the side of the house as Bella's message floated toward Misty. They saw the little bunny's nose twitch. And then, very slowly, the sunshine-yellow of her fluffy coat began to turn exactly the same shade of blue as the toy bunny! At the same time, Bella's magic message faded in the air.

Suddenly, one of the goblins noticed that Misty was bright blue. He could hardly believe his eyes. "Look!" he yelled, jumping up and down. "The bunny turned blue!" He stared suspiciously at the big goblin holding Misty. "What did you do to it?"

"Nothing!" the big goblin snapped. "It's not my fault!"

"Ha, ha!" one of the others laughed smugly. "If Jack Frost wanted a yellow bunny instead of a blue one, you're going to be in big trouble!"

As the goblins began arguing about who'd changed the rabbit's color, Rachel put the toy bunny on the ground. She held onto the other end of the string and turned to Bella.

"Please turn me and Kirsty into fairies again!" she whispered.

soon as Rachel and Kirsty had their wings back, they fluttered up into the air. Kirsty helped Rachel hold the end of the string. The toy bunny was too heavy for Rachel to carry now that she was fairy-size!

"We need Misty to escape and lead the goblins over here," Rachel told Bella.

Bella nodded and began to write in the air with her wand again. This time, the message said:

Rachel, Kirsty, and Bella watched as the message floated around the side of the house toward Misty. The goblins were pushing and shoving one another now. The one with Misty in his arms was so annoyed that he was jumping up and down in anger. The girls could see that he wasn't holding the bunny very tightly anymore.

As soon as Misty saw Bella's message, she began to wriggle and kick. The goblin was taken by surprise! In a second, Misty had squirmed from his grasp and was racing toward the side of the house.

"You klutz!" the other goblins shouted angrily. "You let the bunny go! After it!"

As Misty dashed around the side of the house toward Bella, she began to shrink to fairy-pet–size. Then the tiny blue rabbit scampered up off the ground! She lolloped happily through the air to Bella.

"Good job, Misty!" Bella cried. Rachel and Kirsty smiled as the fairy gave her pet a big hug. "Now come with me!"

As Bella and Misty flew off to hide behind a tree, Rachel turned to Kirsty. "Here come the goblins!" she whispered. "Ready?"

Kirsty nodded.

A few seconds later, the goblins hurtled around the side of the house, grumbling and shouting.

"There she is!" shouted the big goblin, pointing at the toy bunny sitting on the path. "Get her!"

"Head toward the hole, Kirsty!" Rachel whispered.

The two girls began to fly, bouncing the blue bunny on its string along the ground below them. Rachel had been worried that the goblins might be able to see the string, but they couldn't. Their eyes were fixed on the toy rabbit. They charged after it — right toward the hole!

A Magical Easter

Rachel and Kirsty kept flying along,
slowing down a little so that the goblins
could get closer to the bunny. The girls
bounced it carefully onto the twigs and
leaves covering the hole.

"I'm going to catch it!" one of the
goblins yelled triumphantly, reaching out
for the bunny.

"No, let me!" shouted another.

"I want to tell Jack Frost that *I* caught it!" yelled a third.

All four goblins moved to grab the bunny at the same time. They fell on top of the twigs and leaves in a heap. A second later, the covering gave way. Yelping, the goblins all tumbled into the hole. As they did, they pulled the string

out of Rachel's and Kirsty's hands and took the toy bunny with them.

The girls grinned at each other proudly.

"What a great plan, Rachel!" Kirsty cried.

They flew down and hovered over the hole as the goblins inside climbed to their feet.

"Caught in our own trap!" the big goblin groaned.

"It's your fault!" one of the others snapped. "If you hadn't lost the bunny, we wouldn't be here now!"

"At least we got the bunny back!" another added, picking the bunny up. Then he gave a screech of anger. "This isn't the magic bunny — it's a *toy*!"

Rachel and Kirsty laughed as he threw the toy rabbit out of the hole in disgust.

"It's a good thing goblins aren't too smart!" Rachel said.

She and Kirsty flew
over to join Misty and
Bella, who had popped
out from behind the
nearby tree.

"Thank you, girls!"
Bella laughed, her eyes
sparkling with joy. "Misty
is safe, and it's all thanks
to you!"

"We were glad to help," Rachel
replied.

Misty scampered down to Rachel's
shoulder and nuzzled her ear gratefully.
Then the bunny touched her nose to
Kirsty's in thanks.

Suddenly, the tiny rabbit turned to Bella
and began to twitch her nose furiously as
she "talked" to her fairy owner.

"Girls," Bella announced after a moment, "Misty told me she came here because there's a bunny nearby that needs her help. It's lost!"

As Bella was speaking, Kirsty spotted something out of the corner of her eye: a small black bunny was poking its nose out of a nearby bush and staring up at her.

"Rachel, look!" She gasped. "I'm sure that's Jane's bunny. It must have escaped from its box!"

Rachel saw the black rabbit and nodded. "But how did it get out?" she wondered out loud.

"Kids, it's time for presents!" Mrs. Dillon's voice drifted over from the backyard, followed by cheers from the children.

Kirsty looked worried. "We have to get the bunny back into its box before Jane opens it!" she gasped.

"Bella, can you turn us back into girls again?" Rachel asked urgently.

Bella waved her wand right away. As soon as she was back to her normal size, Kirsty tiptoed across the grass toward the black bunny. It stared up at her with big dark eyes. To Kirsty's relief, the bunny let her pick it up.

"Let's go!" Rachel said, grabbing the toy bunny off the ground and untying the string.

Kirsty and Rachel hurried to the garage, while Bella and Misty flew in the air behind them.

The girls could see the children crowding around Mr. and Mrs. Dillon in

the backyard, but luckily, nobody
noticed them.

"Look!" Bella pointed her wand at the
bunny's cardboard box. "That's how
the bunny escaped!"

Rachel and Kirsty looked closer at the
box and saw that a large hole had been
chewed in one side. Carefully, Kirsty
popped the little rabbit
in through the
hole. Then
Bella waved
her wand. A
cloud of dazzling
sparkles swirled
around the box,
making it
whole again.

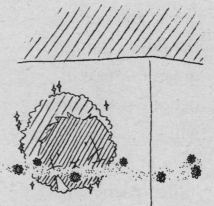

"Time for Jane's special present!" Mr. Dillon announced, heading for the garage.

"Let's get out of here!" Bella whispered.

Quickly, they all hurried out of the garage. They went back to the side gate so they could peek into the yard and watch Jane open her present.

The little girl looked very excited when she saw the box her dad put down on the grass. She pulled the flaps open and gave a squeal of delight. "A bunny! My very own bunny!"

She reached in, gently picked the rabbit up, and gave it a big hug.

"Look!" Kirsty nudged Rachel. "Is that just the sunshine, or can you see a magical sparkle around Jane and her bunny?"

"Definitely a magical sparkle!" Rachel said, grinning.

"I'm going to call it Sooty!" Jane laughed, beaming at her parents.

"Look at Misty!" Kirsty whispered to Rachel.

The magical bunny looked just as happy as Jane. Misty was so thrilled, she was changing to all the different colors of the rainbow, from red to violet.

"It's time for us to go," Bella said,

stroking Misty's fur. "Thanks so much for all your help, girls. Enjoy the rest of the party!"

She blew kisses at them, and Misty twitched her nose — one twitch for Rachel, and one for Kirsty. Then Bella waved her wand. She and Misty disappeared in a shower of fairy dust.

"Time for the chocolate eggs, kids!"
Mrs. Dillon called.

Quickly, Rachel hurried over and
popped the toy bunny back into the
basket of eggs. The children crowded
around Mrs. Dillon
as she handed out
the chocolate.

"The perfect end
to a happy Easter!"
Kirsty said.

Rachel smiled as
she watched the children.
"Yes," she agreed, grinning at Kirsty.
"All the bunnies are with their proper
owners!"

RAINBOW magic
THE PET FAIRIES

Rachel and Kirsty have helped
Katie and Bella find their missing pets.
Now can they help

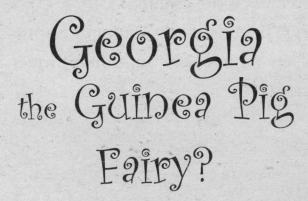

Georgia the Guinea Pig Fairy?

Farmyard Fun

"This must be one of the cutest animals at Strawberry Farm!" Rachel Walker declared, her eyes shining. She stroked the woolly lamb in her arms. "It's so cuddly!"

"And hungry, too," her best friend, Kirsty Tate, added. She tilted up the bottle of milk she was using to feed the lamb, as a farmhand watched. "It almost finished this already!"

Rachel and Kirsty were having a great time at Strawberry Farm! They had already seen a flock of tiny ducklings venturing out for their first swim on the pond. They took a pony ride on a little brown Shetland named Conker. And now they had the chance to hand-feed some of the lambs!

Rachel put the lamb down carefully, and both girls watched it teeter off to join the other lambs in the field.

"I saw a sign for the PET CORNER over there," Rachel said with a meaningful look at Kirsty. "Should we go there next?"

Kirsty smiled at her friend. The two girls shared a wonderful secret: They'd been helping the Pet Fairies all week! Mean Jack Frost had kidnapped the Pet Fairies' seven magical pets, but the pets had managed to escape into the human world. Kirsty knew exactly what Rachel was hoping: Maybe today they'd find another magical pet in the Pet Corner!

RAINBOW magic™

There's Magic in Every Series!

The Rainbow Fairies

The Weather Fairies

The Jewel Fairies

The Pet Fairies

The Fun Day Fairies

The Petal Fairies

The Dance Fairies

Read them all!